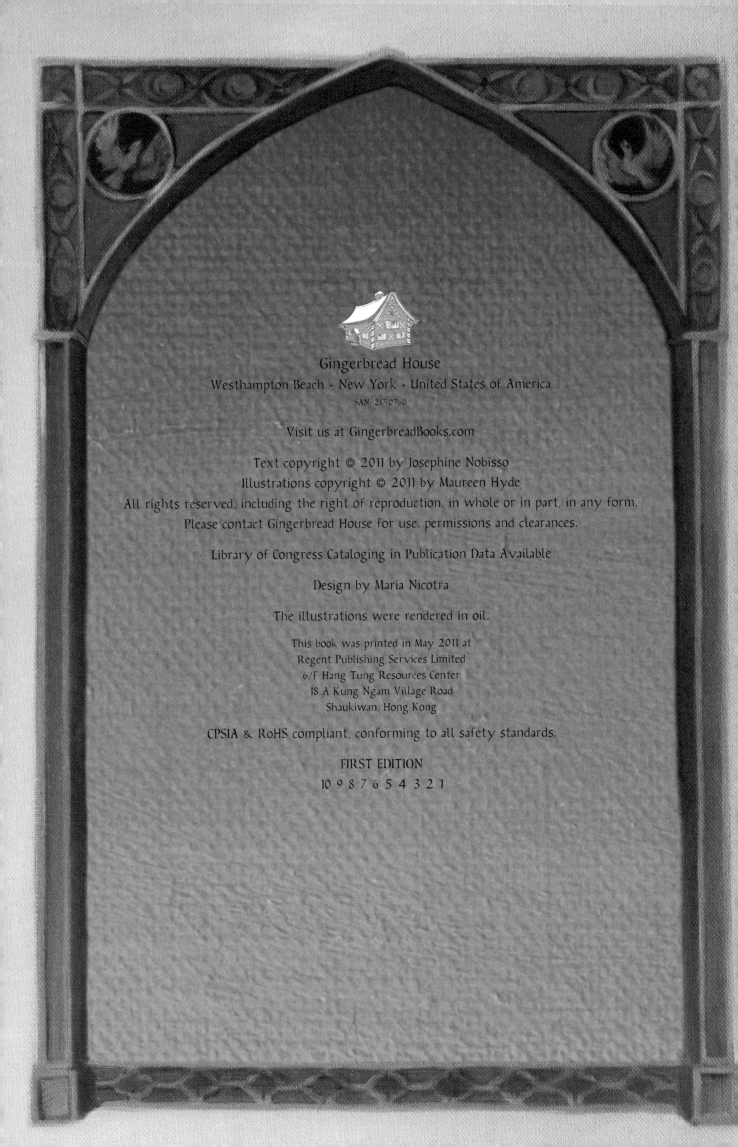

Gingerbread House

Westhampton Beach · New York · United States of America

SAN: 217-0760

Visit us at GingerbreadBooks.com

Library of Congress Cataloging in Publication Data Available

Design by Maria Nicotra

The illustrations were rendered in oil.

This book was printed in May 2011 at
Regent Publishing Services Limited
6/F Hang Tung Resources Center
18 A Kung Ngam Village Road
Shaukiwan, Hong Kong

CPSIA & RoHS compliant, conforming to all safety standards.

FIRST EDITION
10 9 8 7 6 5 4 3 2 1

FRANCIS
Woke Up Early

Josephine Nobisso   Illuminations Maureen Hyde

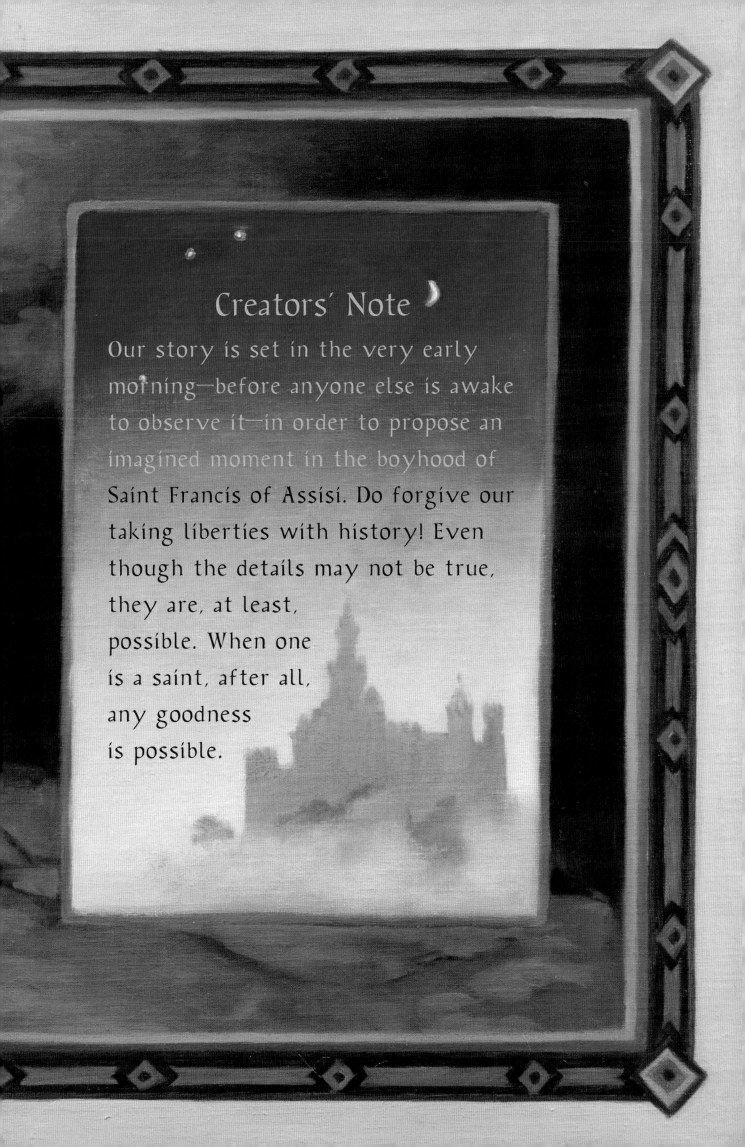

Creators' Note

Our story is set in the very early morning—before anyone else is awake to observe it—in order to propose an imagined moment in the boyhood of Saint Francis of Assisi. Do forgive our taking liberties with history! Even though the details may not be true, they are, at least, possible. When one is a saint, after all, any goodness is possible.

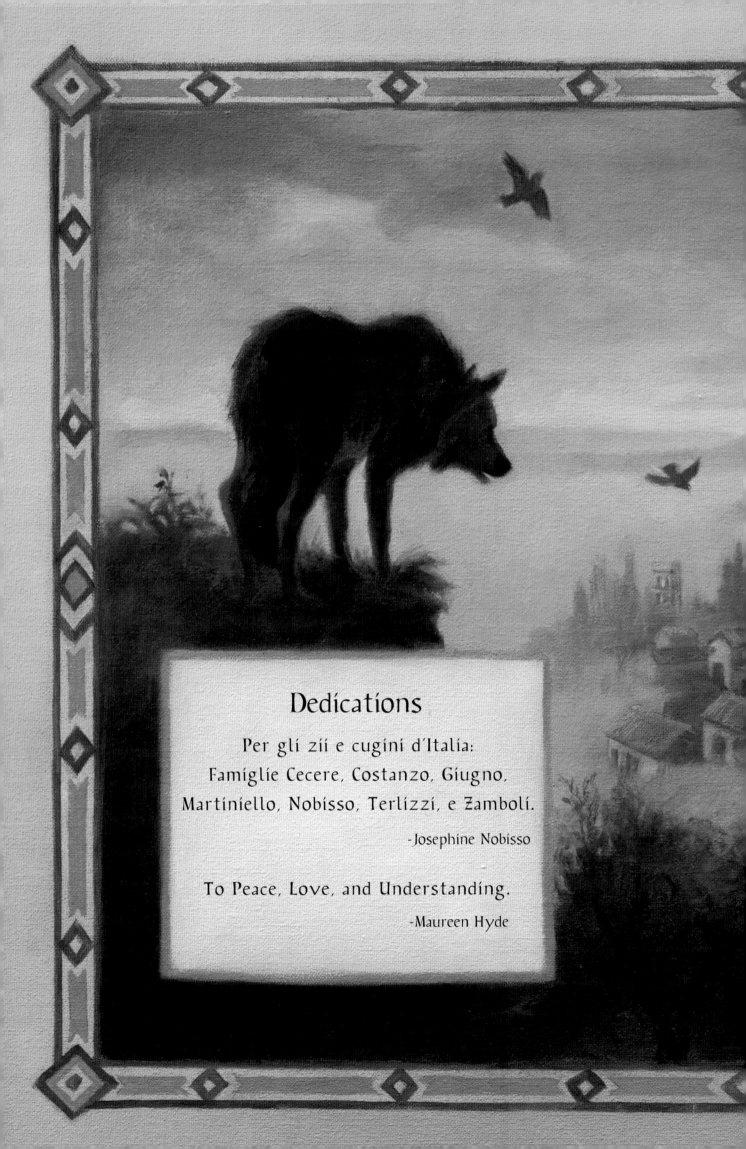

Dedications

Per gli zii e cugini d'Italia:
Famiglie Cecere, Costanzo, Giugno,
Martiniello, Nobisso, Terlizzi, e Zamboli.

-Josephine Nobisso

To Peace, Love, and Understanding.

-Maureen Hyde

Francis woke up early, and covered his Nonna. They had stayed up into the night, listening as all of Assisi discussed the she-wolf that prowled outside the town. "Soon," Francis' Babbo had warned, "she'll get hungry enough to steal into our barnyards and drag the animals away!"

Francis was hungry, himself. He turned his empty breakfast mug right side up. There was always yesterday's bread, but if he had just one egg, and a little bit of fresh goat's milk, all frothy and warm, he could make a breakfast of it, and save the bottom—the best—for Nonna!

Francis knelt at his window,
crumbling some of the bread into his palms.
And when the birds saw that their friend was
already up, calls of joy filled the hills as they
flitted into town. The birds bustled into Francis'
hands, their twiggy feet pinching, their horn-like
beaks swiping left and right.

In the barnyard at the bottom of the hill,
the horses snorted in greeting, stamping
in their stalls, so that steam and dust
billowed from the barn windows.

A breeze slammed the stable door shut,
and the goat kid bleated out to Francis
before scampering under his mother,
who huddled him against the wall.

In the courtyard below, the rooster strutted
around his hens, flexing his claws and
creaking like a rusty hinge.

An idea occurred to Francis. If he worked
fast enough, he could secure the animals
in the barnyard, collect that breakfast, and
be back before anyone in the house was up!

Francis scurried past his sleeping Mamma, and past his Babbo, draped over a worktable, like more cloth.

He hurried past the kitchen maid and the cat, snoring at
the hearth, and slid back the bolt of the timber door.

The hens flapped around the boy. They
squawked as he urged them, dashing
over stones thick as monks' books.

Delicate butterflies fluttered about Francis' head, silent pastel confetti keeping company as child and chickens tripped and flitted downhill through flowers growing wild and grasses wet with dew.

But when Francis stumbled at the bottom of the hill, he landed right in the shadow of...

...the wolf.

The hens, suddenly quiet, clustered close.

Francis swallowed hard, and stood up.
He led the chickens into their coop,
and collected not one egg, but two.

Outside, Francis spied the wolf's shadow,
low and wide, crouching. The animal
had waited for him.

Francis sprinted to the goat pen
where the nanny butted the backs
of his knees, and her kid nuzzled
a moist, "Maaa!" into his palm.

The boy opened their slammed door,
and the three of them scampered inside.

Francis milked the nanny then,
filling a crock, all frothy and warm.

The horses whinnied and stamped as the wolf's shadow
moved over the boy's shoulders, but Francis reassured

them as he broke one of the eggs into a stone bowl,
and poured out some of the milk.

Francis carried the bowl to the base of the hill,
away from the barnyard. Soon, the wolf's shadow
seeped around him, from behind. Francis turned then,
and the sight of that wolf—huge and beautiful—made
his breath catch. Her intelligent eyes flitted, as though
wanting to speak. She pulled back her magnificent
head, muscular ears nimbly twitching, listening,
because now, the child was speaking to her.

"I've prepared a little breakfast for you, Sister Wolf!"
Francis was saying.

The animal sniffed the air, daintily lifting one
paw as the boy laid the bowl on the ground.

"And if you decide to behave..!" he added.

Francis began the climb toward home, the morning sun slowing him. Suddenly, the wolf sidled up beside the boy, so that he found his elbow leaning on her bony back. And on that perch, Francis fairly floated uphill, through poppies and daisies and lilies growing wild.

When they reached Francis' kitchen door,
the animal bounded onto a rise and looked the
town over. Licking milk from her jowls, she turned.
Wolf and child gently studied each other. Francis
smiled, and passing through the wolf's shadow,
he let himself into the sleeping house.

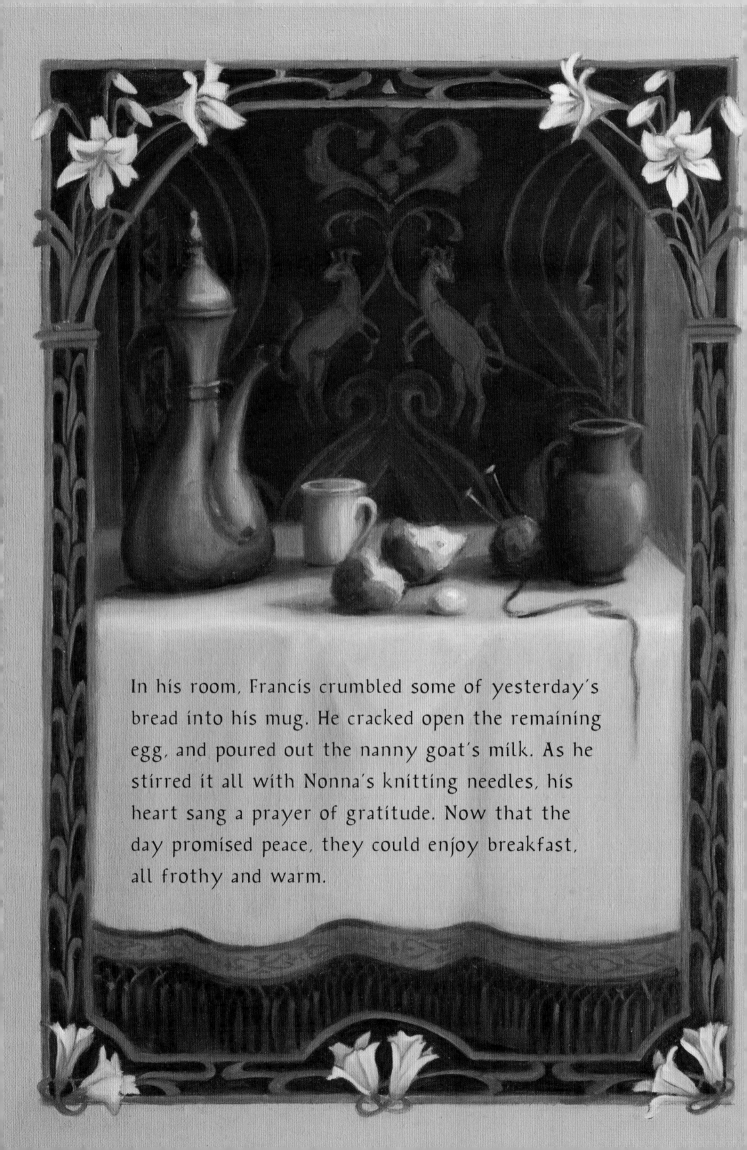

In his room, Francis crumbled some of yesterday's bread into his mug. He cracked open the remaining egg, and poured out the nanny goat's milk. As he stirred it all with Nonna's knitting needles, his heart sang a prayer of gratitude. Now that the day promised peace, they could enjoy breakfast, all frothy and warm.

Author's Postscript

Although something is known about Saint Francis of Assisi as a youth, and much is understood about the stigmatist's great sanctity as an adult, precious little has been revealed about the childhood of this Giovanni Francesco Bernadone.

When, in the 1980's, the artist Maureen Hyde asked if I would create a fiction on that hidden subject, my fancy flew to two famous and astonishing incidents: that of the Saint's having converted the fierce wolf of Gubbio, and that of his having delivered a sermon to a multitude of most appreciative birds of varied species.

Maureen's request parted the veil, so that I squinted into the Italian sunshine of my memory, to draw upon my own girlhood impressions during field trips to Assisi and Gubbio, while I was a student in Urbino. I wondered: how do saints gain dominion over nature, which is often—especially when it is wild—separated from man? Fallen Creation seems to draw its very dignity from a sense that it will one day be restored to its original state. I reasoned that, in Francesco d'Assisi the creatures must have recognized that,

somehow, Eden was made present on Earth. If mankind waits in joyful hope for the coming of the Kingdom, when peace will be perfectly re-established, wouldn't other creatures happily subject themselves to a saint who already does the Will of God in such full measure?

And what, I wondered, would a moment with that saint, as a boy, look like?

With the resultant text in hand, Maureen traveled to Assisi several times, to apply her own vision and skill to oil paintings that seem to give off the very fragrances and sounds of a world Francis knew. Over two decades and two continents, the canvases moved from studio to studio, where, sometimes, the artist set up elaborate stretches of string to capture perspectives. Since the time we first started this project, many a children's picture book has appeared about St. Francis of Assisi. None of them, however, has speculated on the boy he might have been—a boy who conquered the hearts of beasts because his own heart had already been conquered by Divine Love.